Miss Bindergarten Celebrates the Last Day of Kindergarten

by JOSEPH SLATE

illustrated by ASHLEY WOLFF

PUFFIN BOOKS

PUFFIN BOOKS
Published by the Penguin Group
Penguin Young Readers Group, 345 Hudson Street, New York, New York 10014, U.S.A.
Penguin Group (Canada), 90 Eglinton Avenue East, Suite 700, Toronto, Ontario, Canada M4P 2Y3
(a division of Pearson Penguin Canada Inc.)
Penguin Books Ltd, 80 Strand, London WC2R 0RL, England
Penguin Ireland, 25 St Stephen's Green, Dublin 2, Ireland (a division of Penguin Books Ltd)
Penguin Group (Australia), 250 Camberwell Road, Camberwell, Victoria 3124, Australia
(a division of Pearson Australia Group Pty Ltd)
Penguin Books India Pvt Ltd, 11 Community Centre, Panchsheel Park, New Delhi - 110 017, India
Penguin Group (NZ), 67 Apollo Drive, Rosedale, North Shore 0632, New Zealand (a division of Pearson New Zealand Ltd)
Penguin Books (South Africa) (Pty) Ltd, 24 Sturdee Avenue, Rosebank, Johannesburg 2196, South Africa

Registered Offices: Penguin Books Ltd, 80 Strand, London WC2R 0RL, England

First published in the United States of America by Dutton Children's Books, a division of Penguin Young Readers Group, 2005
Published by Puffin Books, a division of Penguin Young Readers Group, 2008

1 3 5 7 9 10 8 6 4 2

HERSHEY'S KISSES is a registered trademark of Hershey Chocolate & Confectionery Corp.
Text copyright © Joseph Slate, 2005
Illustrations copyright © Ashley Wolff, 2005
All rights reserved

THE LIBRARY OF CONGRESS HAS CATALOGED THE DUTTON CHILDREN'S BOOKS EDITION AS FOLLOWS:
Slate, Joseph.
Miss Bindergarten celebrates the last day of kindergarten / by Joseph Slate ; illustrated by Ashley Wolff. p. cm.
Summary: Miss Bindergarten and her class celebrate the last day of kindergarten with a party and good wishes.
ISBN: 978-0-525-47744-0 (hc)
[1. Kindergarten—Fiction. 2. Schools—Fiction. 3. Teachers—Fiction.]
I. Wolff, Ashley, ill. II. Title.
PZ7.S6289Mh 2005 [E]—dc22 2005009448

Puffin Books ISBN 978-0-14-241060-8
Manufactured in China

oval

star

THE

BE PREPARED FOR ANYTHING

HAVE FUN!

circle

I LOVE KIDS

hexagon

Join Mr. Mack's
SUMMER
READING ROUNDTABLE
• Contests
• Prizes
• Pajama Party
in the library!

Miss Fiona's
Swimming Class
call: 524-3952
www.mmm.com
Come on in, the water's fine!

For Becky Watson of Camp Hill, Alabama, and all the kindergarten teachers who contributed ideas for this book. And the children who wanted it. —J.S.

My heartfelt thanks to Joe and to all the generous kindergarten teachers and students who helped me bring these books to life. —A.W.

**It's the last day
of kindergarten,
and—
oh, oh, oh!—**

Adam brings carnations.

Christopher says,
"It's for Miss B—
a big goodbye balloon."

Brenda has perfume.

the last day of kindergarten.

Danny scrubs a table.

Emily hands back rocks.

Franny clears her bin and shouts,
"Oh no—three smelly socks!"

Miss Bindergarten celebrates

the last day of kindergarten.

Gwen collects the building blocks.

Henry packs them away

Ian hides beneath the desk.
"I really want to stay."

the last day of kindergarten.

Jessie shows off her bathing suit.

Matty sets up a sprinkler. Noah connects the hose.

Ophelia tries to take a drink
and gets squirted in the nose.

Miss Bindergarten celebrates

the last day of kindergarten.

Patricia passes pizza.

Quentin says, "Cheese, please."

Raffie's pepperoni slices balance on his knees.

Miss Bindergarten celebrates

the last day of kindergarten.

Sara signs a memory book.

Tommy prints "Good luck."

Ursula tells about their trip to see a fire truck.

avier gets a ribbon
for perfect class attendance.

the last day of kindergarten.

Yolanda yells, "We love you!"

Zach gives a cheer.

"Goodbye, kindergarten," says Miss B.
"It's been a special year."

"**H**ere's a little gift for you,
a penny and a Kiss.

The penny for success to come,
the Kiss that you'll be missed."

Miss Bindergarten says

goodbye to kindergarten.